the ugliest dog in the world

by James Holding, Jr.

pictures by Marilyn Miller

Xerox Education Publications

Text copyright © 1979 by James Holding, Jr.
Illustrations copyright © 1979 by Marilyn Miller

Publishing, Executive and Editorial Offices:
Xerox Education Publications
Middletown, Connecticut 06457

ISBN 0-88375-219-0
Library of Congress Catalog Card Number: 78-78365

Once there was a dog named Algernon.
He was very ugly. His head was too big for his
body. He had a short, thick neck and short, stubby
legs. He had a flat, wrinkled, smashed-in-looking
face with a black smashed-in nose. And some of
his lower teeth stuck out in plain sight, even when
his mouth was closed.

Algernon belonged to a little girl named
Caroline, who called him Algy for short. Caroline
was eight years old and had long black hair. Algy's
hair was just the opposite: short and white.

Caroline didn't think Algy was ugly. She thought he was a lovely dog. She petted him and fed him and bathed him and loved him dearly. And Algy loved Caroline, too.

All the same, Algy wasn't happy. He wasn't satisfied just to be Caroline's pet. He longed for people to respect and admire him. He wanted to be a success. He wanted to amount to something.

Surely, he thought, there must be some secret of success that I don't know about. If I could only find out what it is, I'll bet I could really amount to something!

Suddenly Algy had an idea. I'll ask my friends about it, he decided.

He went to see a lady poodle who lived nearby. She was older than Algy and her name was Madame Belle. She was lying on a velvet pillow with her eyes closed.

Algy squatted down beside her and said politely into her ear, "Madame Belle, will you tell me the secret of success? You must know what it is, because you've been on TV several times."

Madame Belle opened one eye. "Hello, Algy," she yawned. "Why do you want to know the secret of success?"

"So that I can *amount* to something," answered Algy.

Madame Bell opened her other eye and looked at Algy's smashed-in face. "The secret of success," she said, "is beauty, Algy. Beauty. Like mine."

"I was afraid that was it," said Algy.

"You must have your coat clipped just so," Madame Belle went on. "You must carry yourself as proudly as a queen. You must be so beautiful that you always win the blue ribbon at the dog show, Algy. Like me." Madame Belle stood up and posed so that Algy could see how beautiful she was.

"I'm afraid I'm not very beautiful," Algy
sighed.

Madame Belle was sympathetic. "You could
try wearing a red ribbon around your neck, Algy.
Or smooth out those wrinkles in your face with
wrinkle cream. And if you could only hide some of
those ugly teeth!"

Algy went home and looked at himself in the mirror on Caroline's bedroom door. And he knew that even if he tried everything Madame Belle had told him, he'd still be the ugliest dog in the world.

Several days later, he was taking an early morning walk through the fields near Caroline's house when he came upon a large dog who was standing as still as a statue in a very funny position. His nose was stretched straight out in front of him, pointing to a bush. His tail was held straight out behind him. And one of his forepaws was lifted off the ground as though he had a sore foot.

"Hello," said Algy to this strange dog. "Why are you standing like that, so stiff and still?"

"I'm pointing, silly," said the strange dog.

"What are you pointing at?" asked Algy.

"At the birds in that bush," said the dog. "I'm a hunting dog, don't you see? When I find birds, I show my master where they are by pointing at them like this."

"Birds?" said Algy. He looked at the bush. "I don't see any birds."

"They're there, all the same," said the hunting dog. "Go over to the bush and bark if you don't believe me."

Algy ran to the bush and barked. A whole family of quail burst out of the bush and flew away.

"See?" said the hunting dog.

"How did you know the birds were there?" asked Algy.

"I *smelled* them. I've got an extra good smeller for finding birds, you see. That's what you've got to have if you want to be a success. An extra good smeller."

"Thanks for telling me," cried Algy. "I'm going right home and try out *my* smeller. I hope it's an extra good one, so I can amount to something like you."

But poor Algy was no good at smelling, either. He almost had to stand on his head to get his flat nose close enough to the ground to smell anything at all.

Well, he thought, maybe there is more than one secret of success. If I can't be beautiful, and I can't have an extra good smeller, maybe there's another way I can amount to something.

That night, when it was very dark, Algy heard a sound far up in the air over his head. What he heard was the wind whistling through the feathers of his old friend, the great horned owl, as the owl flew over Algy's doghouse. In a minute or two, the owl called "Whoo! Whoo! Whoo!" from the live oak tree at the end of the yard.

Algy trotted to the tree and looked up into its branches. "Good evening, Owl," he said. "Do you mind if I ask you a question?"

"Whoo, whoo, whoo is it?" hooted the owl. He knew perfectly well that it was Algy speaking to him, but he liked to make jokes.

Algy said, "Caroline says you are the wisest bird in the world, Owl. Would you mind telling me the secret of success?"

"It's quite simple, Algy," said the owl, clicking his powerful beak. "The trick is, if you want to be a wise and successful citizen in this world, you have to be able to see in the dark."

Algy was surprised. "See in the dark?" he repeated. "Whatever for?"

"Ah," said the owl, "if you can see in the dark, the world lies at your feet. You're the ruler of the roost, Algy, because you can see all kinds of things that nobody else can see."

"Could I learn to see in the dark?" asked Algy.

"I certainly hope so," said the owl, "for that's the key to success." And he flew away in search of his dinner.

Algy squinted his eyes, and blinked, and strained to see the owl in the darkness, but he couldn't see a thing. "I guess I'll never be able to see in the dark," he said to himself sadly.

The next day, Algy happened to meet his friend Silver Streak, a greyhound. "Silver," said Algy in a troubled voice, "I'm trying to find the secret of success. I've asked several friends about it, and each one gives me a different answer. I know you're a great success because Caroline saw your picture in the newspaper. Won't you please tell me what your secret is?"

14

"Sure," said Silver Streak. "The secret of success is *speed*, Algy. You've got to be very, very fast on your feet if you want to amount to anything. Take me, for example. I'm the fastest runner in the whole state of Florida. I win more dog races than anybody. So develop your footwork, Algy, if you want to be a big success." And Silver Streak bounded away on his long, slim legs so fast that he was out of sight in less than a minute.

"So *that's* it," said Algy to himself. "Speed." He ran home as fast as he could. His short legs sped over the ground. He strained every muscle to run fast. But it was no good. He couldn't run half as fast as Silver Streak.

By the time he got home, he was tired and out of breath and very thirsty. He went into the kitchen to get a drink of water. And there was Dickie, Caroline's canary bird, in his cage near the window.

Between laps at the cool water in his dish, Algy said, "Dickie, everyone thinks you're a wonderful fellow. Even though you're quite tiny, and a funny yellow color, and never leave your cage. Can you tell me why you're such a success?"

"It's true," chirped Dickie in a high sweet voice, "that I'm tiny, and yellow, and live in a cage. But I can *sing*, Algy, I can sing! That's the secret of success. You must be able to sing to amount to anything. Why don't you try it?"

Algy raised his chin and tried to sing. But all that came out of his mouth was a kind of half-bark, half-moan that sounded as though somebody were hitting an empty barrel with a stick.

"Stop! Stop!" shouted Dickie. "That's enough, Algy! You're a terrible singer. I'm sorry."

Algy was sorry, too. He sulked around the house for days after that, wearing a sad expression. He lost his appetite. He wouldn't play with Caroline. Caroline thought he was sick.

That's why she asked her parents to allow Algy to go with them on their summer vacation to Uncle Jerry's farm in the country. "Algy will get well quickly on the farm," Caroline said eagerly. "Let's take him with us."

So Algy went to Uncle Jerry's farm with Caroline and her family in their station wagon. Algy rode in back with the luggage, never dreaming that on Uncle Jerry's farm he would find the secret of success.

It happened the very next day. "Come on, Algy," said Caroline after breakfast, "let's take a walk."

Through the farmyard they went, past the barn, past the chicken house, past the pigpens, and down the lane between the orange grove and the tomato field to the wide pastures beyond. Soon they came to a pasture with a barbed-wire fence around it.

"Oh, Algy, look at those flowers!" said
Caroline, pointing to the daisies and buttercups
growing in the pasture. "I'm going to pick a bunch
for Mother." She lay down on her stomach and
wiggled under the lowest strand of barbed wire into
the pasture. Algy wiggled through after her.
Caroline began to pick flowers. Algy ran off to sniff
at a rabbit burrow nearby.

Suddenly, Algy heard Caroline scream.

Algy looked around. A huge bull with curving horns was pawing the ground not twenty feet away from Caroline! The bull's hoarse bellows filled the air. He was very, very angry, that was plain.

Algy said to him, "What's the matter, bull? Why are you so angry?"

"Why am I so angry?" snorted the bull. "Isn't this *my* pasture? Aren't those *my* flowers that nosey little girl in the red dress is picking? I'm going to teach her a lesson she'll never forget!" The bull raised his tail and lowered his head and charged at Caroline, ready to hook her with his sharp horns and toss her over the fence.

Caroline couldn't move for a second, she was so frightened. But when the bull began to rush toward her, she leaped to her feet, dropped her wildflowers, and began to run. "Algy!" she shrieked, just once. Then she was too busy running to say anything else.

Algy knew what he had to do. He had to stop that charging bull somehow. And an old instinct from long, long ago told him exactly how to do it.

He shot like a bullet into the path of the bull. He gathered himself on his short, stubby legs. Then he leaped straight for the bull's nose! He felt his big, sharp teeth bite through the tender flesh of the bull's nostrils. His jaws snapped shut with a click.

The bull bellowed in pain. He slid to a stop, his eyes wild. He forgot all about Caroline. All he could think of was this strange creature clinging to his nose. He swung his huge head from side to side, trying to make Algy let go. But Algy hung on.

Caroline scraped her knees and tore her pretty red dress as she slid under the pasture fence to safety. She scrambled to her feet, thinking Algy would be right behind her.

But he wasn't. Algy was still in the pasture,
clinging tightly and ever more tightly to the bull's
nose. Up and down, back and forth, with mighty
jerks of his powerful head, the bull swung Algy like
a leaf in a windstorm. Yet Algy hung on bravely,
with all his might, his jaws clamped, his eyes
bulging with the effort.

And right then,
at that terrible moment,
a very strange thing
happened: Algy
found the
secret of
success.

For he suddenly realized that he *couldn't* let go of the bull's nose, even if he'd wanted to! His lower teeth made an unbreakable lock with his upper ones—and the only thing that could make them loosen their grip was for the bull to stop pulling against them.

He found out something else too: that his flat, smashed-in nose was shaped just exactly right to let him breathe through it perfectly while he hung onto the bull with his teeth.

Oh, my! thought Algy as he battled the huge
bull, *this* is why my teeth stick out, *this* is why my
nose is flat and smashed-in, *this* is why I'm so ugly!
So that I can stop this bull from hurting Caroline!

The bull's bellows grew weaker. Soon they
stopped altogether. Then the bull stopped jerking
Algy every which way. And finally, tired out and
helpless, the bull stood quietly with his great head
drooping and waited patiently for Algy to stop
biting his nose.

When the bull stopped moving his head, Algy
could unlock his jaws. He pulled his teeth out of
the bull's nose and scrambled quickly under the
fence to join Caroline, who had watched the whole
thing. "Oh, Algy!" cried Caroline, throwing her

arms about Algy's neck, "You're the bravest dog there ever was!"

Algy wheezed and panted with pleasure and licked Caroline's chin. He was very happy. Because now he knew, without any doubt, that he amounted to something, after all.

Even if he *was* the ugliest dog in the world.